When is Saturday?

Featuring Jim Henson's Sesame Street Muppets

By DEBORAH KOVACS

Illustrated by
RICHARD BROWN

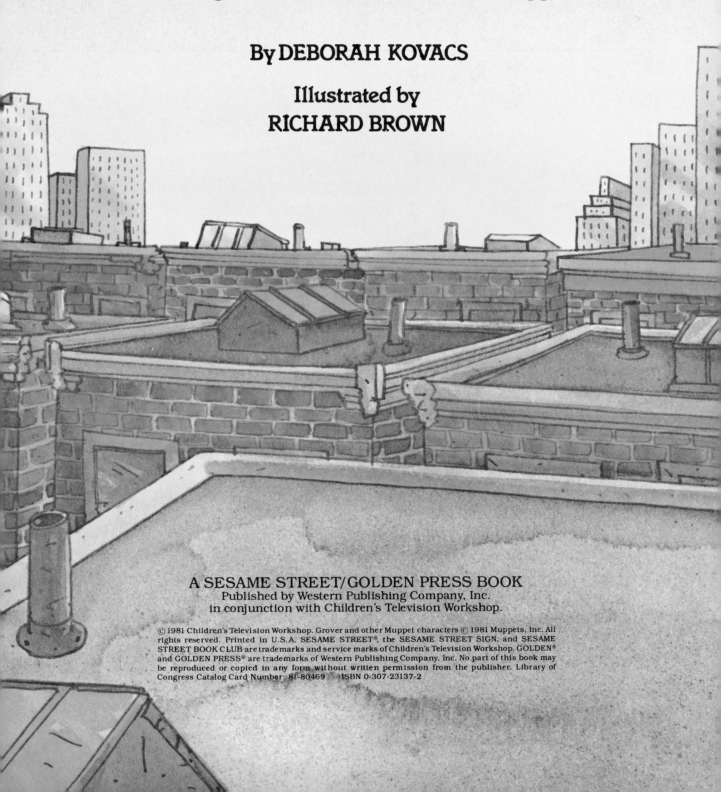

A SESAME STREET/GOLDEN PRESS BOOK
Published by Western Publishing Company, Inc.
in conjunction with Children's Television Workshop.

SUNDAY

It was a quiet Sunday and Grover was bored. "There's nothing to do around here," he said. "Nothing exciting ever happens."

"But, Grover," said his mommy. "Something exciting is going to happen. Your Uncle Georgie is coming to visit us on Saturday!"

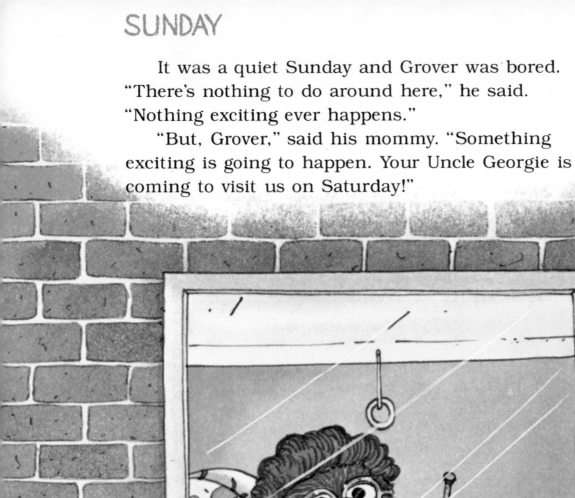

"Saturday? That is *very* exciting!" said Grover. "I can hardly wait to show him my new bed, and take him to the zoo, and..." Grover stopped. "But when *is* Saturday, Mommy?" he asked. "Is tomorrow Saturday?"

"No, Grover," said his mommy. "Saturday is a week away. Today is Sunday. After that comes Monday, Tuesday, Wednesday, Thursday, Friday, and *then* Saturday."

"Oh, my!" said Grover. "That is too many days for me to remember. How will I know when it is going to be Saturday?"

Grover's mommy made him a calendar. It showed all the days of the week. She drew a circle around Saturday. "Let's put this calendar on the wall," she said. "We'll cross out each day when it's over. That way you can always see how many days are left until Saturday."

Before going to bed that night Grover crossed out Sunday on his calendar. "Today was Sunday," he said to himself. "Five more days until Saturday."

MONDAY

The next morning Grover looked at his calendar. "Today is Monday," he said. "Monday is housecleaning day." He helped his mother do the cleaning. Then he made a little tent-house, and he cleaned that, too.

On Monday afternoon Grover, Prairie Dawn and
Herry Monster made animals out of clay. Herry
Monster made a clay kitten. Prairie Dawn made a big
clay dragon. Grover made a clay cow.

On Monday night Grover drew another X on his calendar. "Today was Monday," he thought as he went to bed. "Four more days until Saturday."

TUESDAY

On Tuesday Grover went to the store with his mother. They bought lots of vegetables to make a big pot of soup.

That night Grover made another X on his calendar. "Tuesday was vegetable soup day," he said. "Only three more days until Saturday."

WEDNESDAY

On Wednesday Grover went to Ernie and Bert's house to play. They made a building with blocks.

Wednesday afternoon Ernie and Bert and Grover went to the library with Big Bird. It was Story Day. They heard a story called "Rumplestiltskin." Grover loved it.

That night, as Grover made an X on Wednesday, he said, "Wednesday was Story Day. Only two more days until Saturday."

THURSDAY

On Thursday Grover played jump rope with Herry Monster and Cookie Monster. Grover jumped 53 times without missing!

Cookie Monster and Grover went to Grover's house afterwards. Grover's mother let them play with some old clothes. They played dress-up all afternoon.

Grover's mother said, "Why don't you ask Cookie Monster to stay overnight tonight?"

"Oh, Mommy!" said Grover. "What a wonderful idea!"

Just before they went to sleep, Grover made another X on his calendar. "Thursday Cookie came to stay," he said happily. "One more day until Saturday."

FRIDAY

Friday was the day Grover's mommy always took him to the park. Grover played on the slide with Cookie Monster. He pushed Big Bird on the swings. Then Big Bird pushed him.

Then they all went to Grover's house and had cookies and milk.

On Friday night, as Grover made an X on his calendar, he said, "Friday was park day. Tomorrow is Saturday. Oh, my goodness! No more days until Saturday. Uncle Georgie will be here tomorrow. I think I will make up a little poem to surprise him."

SATURDAY

Grover woke up early on Saturday. He looked at his calendar. "Today is the day," he said. "Uncle Georgie is coming."

He hurried into the kitchen for breakfast.

Just as Grover and his mommy were finishing their cereal, the doorbell rang.

It was Uncle Georgie! Grover was so happy to see him! "Hello, Uncle Georgie!" Grover shouted, giving him a big hug.

"Hello, Grover!" said Uncle Georgie, giving him just as big a hug. "What have you been doing?"

"I have learned something new," said Grover. "And I made up a poem to tell you about it."

"My poem is called 'The Days of the Week.'

"Sunday, Monday,
  Do I know another?
  Yes I do! Tuesday!
  No need to ask my mother.
  Next comes Wednesday,
  I am sure of that.
  After which comes Thursday,
  I will give myself a pat.
  The next day is Friday,
  I can say the days out loud!
  And the last day is Saturday,
  Oh, I am so proud."